BORIS
and the
Wrong Shadow

NAME ....

TYPE OF SHADOW

BOY   ☐   GIRL   ☐

MONSTER   ☐   FISH   ☐

BUTTERFLY   ☐   OTHER

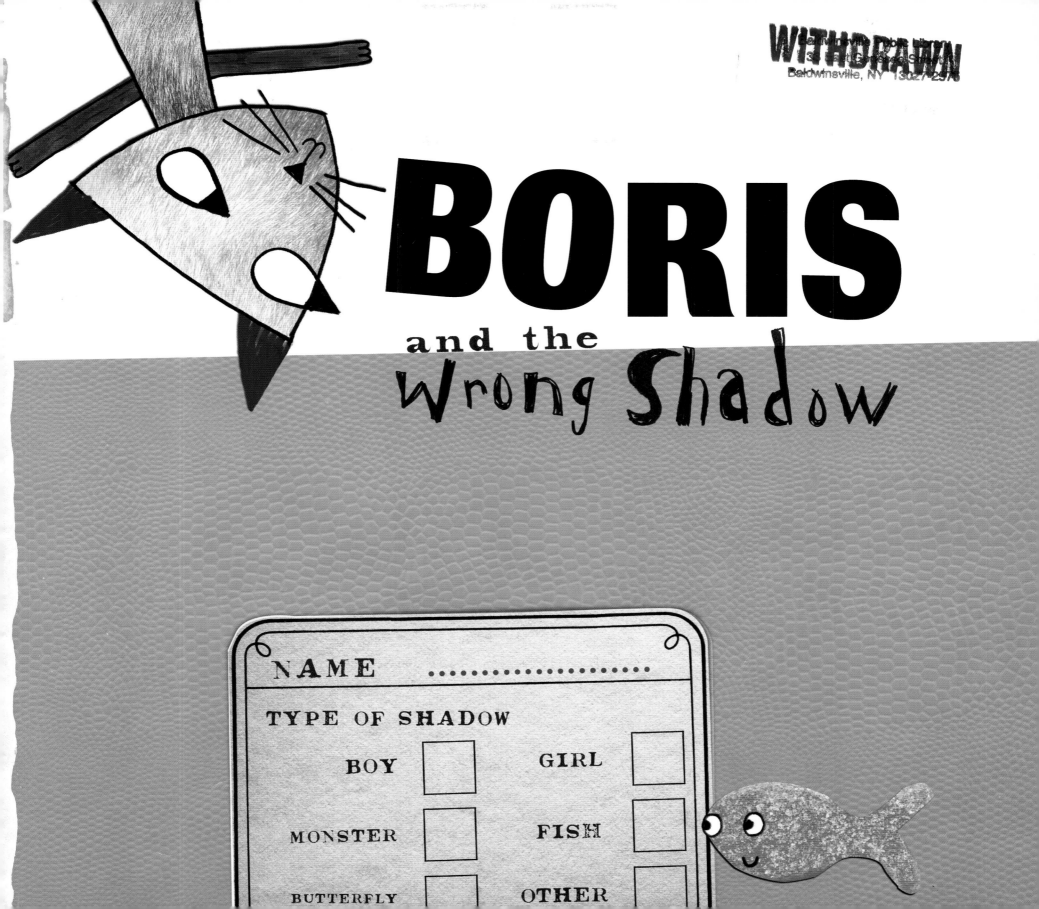

FOR the **TWO** Hodgkinsons

WHO are (without a S H A D O W of a doubt)

SHINY & BRIGHT (FACT).

OCT 1 2 2008

tiger tales
an imprint of ME Media, LLC
202 Old Ridgefield Road, Wilton, CT 06897
Published in the United States 2009
Originally published in Great Britain 2008
by Orchard Books
a division of Hachette Children's Books,
an Hachette Livre UK Company
Text and illustrations copyright ©2008 Leigh Hodgkinson
CIP data is available
ISBN-13: 978-1-58925-082-6
ISBN-10: 1-58925-082-6
Printed in China

BORIS

and the
Wrong Shadow

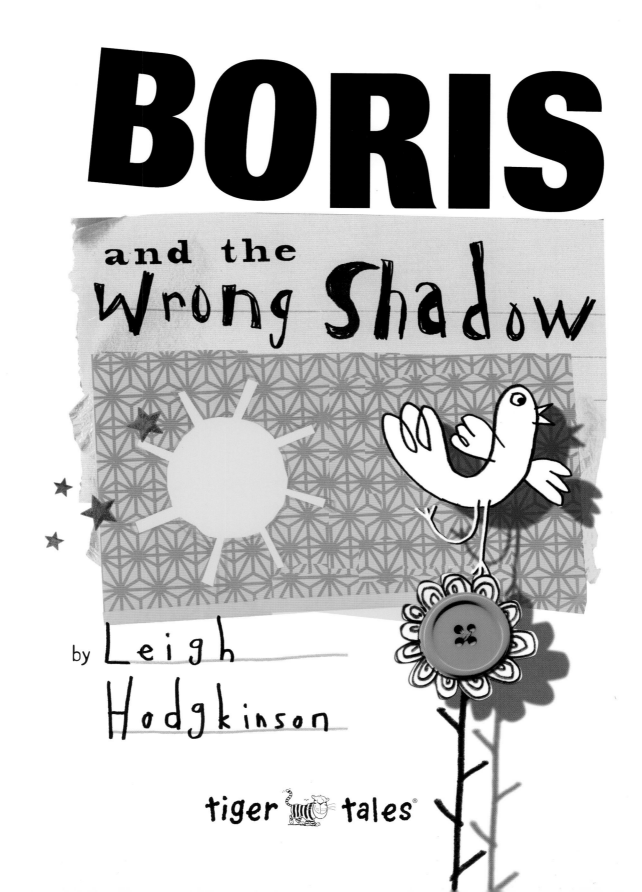

by Leigh Hodgkinson

tiger tales

Boris

has just woken up from his catnap. He smiles as he remembers his dream…

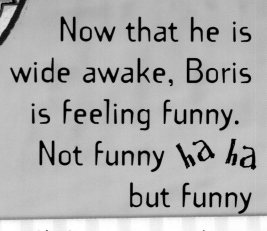

swimming

in a **gigantic** bowl of creamy milk.

Now that he is wide awake, Boris is feeling funny. Not funny ha ha but funny STRANGE.

Boris has a feeling that things aren't quite as they should be.

For some reason, Boris appears to have the

Wrong shadow.

He has no idea why, but Boris decides not to let a silly thing like this...

spoil an otherwise pleasant afternoon.

As it turns out, Boris's afternoon is NOT at all pleasant. The other cats snicker.

Little Flossy Fluffball SQUEAKS at him.

The beaky birds
don't **bother** to look
up from their

SPLASHY bath.

Boris is starting to wonder if he **actually** is a **mouse** after all?

He does like the **odd** nibble of cheese, if that means anything.

Boris thinks that if he had any other shadow—

PERHAPS something
with a little more

WOW!

—everything would be HUNKY-DORY.

BUT it isn't in the least bit

hunky-dory.

Not in the slightest.

HOWEVER,

even GLOOMY cats need to stretch their legs occasionally. Perfect timing, too, as this is when Boris spies something VERY interesting indeed . . .

Boris asks VERY politely if Vernon took his shadow.

Vernon says,

"NO. Not exactly."

Boris thinks that SOMEONE is telling a tiny lie.

Vernon gulps and says, "While you were snoozing, your shadow got BORED and FIDGETY and wandered off."

Hmmmmm.

Boris would really like the
switch-SWAP switched BACK!

VERNON thinks that RIGHT NOW would probably be a good time to scurry home.

UH-OH!

Boris's shadow is far too **BIG** to fit through the door.

Vernon squishes, SQUEEZES, and SQUASHES it —

but it JUST WON'T BUDGE!

then **WHAT** IS THE **POINT?**

You see it's JUST not EASY
being a tiny pink mouse
all of the time.

Having Boris's
MARVELOUS shadow
meant that **EVERYBODY**
took Vernon seriously
for a change.

"You couldn't
POSSIBLY ever
understand, Boris,"

he squeaks oh-so quietly.

Boris knows **EXACTLY** how it feels, as it happens.

It's not nice to be **snickered** at, **SQUEAKED** at, and **IGNORED**, you know.

It made Boris feel TERRIBLY small and all alone.

Perhaps if they BOTH stopped worrying about silly shadows, they could concentrate on more important things—like

having fun together!

First things first, to get Vernon out of this pickle!

Vernon PUSHEs

The shadow

until suddenly . . .

PING!

TOPPILY

and Boris **PULLS.**

STRETCHES like a giant rubber band...

tumble,

thunkety bump.

PHEW-EE! Not exactly easy-peasy,

Vernon is loving being footloose and fancy-free again

and has a new SPRING in his step.

This is because being with BOTH his own shadow AND Boris means DOUBLE the fun!

Now, Vernon feels even

BETTER

than a SUPERSTAR.

More like a

SUPER-DUPER
STAR!

And to be honest,
lugging that big, bulky
shadow around was a touch tiring.

Now, that is what Boris calls a pretty perfect plan!
One slurpy sip later, Boris clambers up onto his favorite pillow.

This time his shadow
is sleepy **too** and
sticking like glue,
so there will be

NO

prowling around

and getting into
trouble
with a certain

mischievous

little

mouse.